How Do Dinosaurs Say

I'M MAD?

BEIPIAOSAURUS

PACHYRHINOSAURU

SAUROPELTA

AFROVENATOR

BARAPASAURUS

SAUROLOPHUS

SCAPHOGNATHUS

ALBERTOSAURUS

THECODONT

LYSTROSAURUS

BEIPIAOSAURUS

PACHYRHINOSAURUS

SAUROPELTA

AFROVENATOR

BARAPASAURUS

SCAPHOGNATHUS

SAUROLOPHUS

ALBERTOSAURUS

LYSTROSAURUS

THECODONT

JANE YOLEN

How Do Dinosaurs Say

I'M MAD?

Illustrated by
MARK TEAGUE

SCHOLASTIC INC.

Everybody gets angry sometimes. Kids do. So do parents. Sometimes we get
angry when we're scared, or want something we can't have, or are feeling mean
or feeling sick. Anger can be very frightening, and it can make people sad. But
there are lots of ways to learn how to control anger, just as the dinosaurs do
in this book. Some of them count to ten, some of them have a time out, and
some of them take deep breaths. Then, when the dinosaurs are calm again, they
clean up any mess they've made, they say, "I'm sorry," and they give big hugs.
Just as you do.

This book was originally published in hardcover by The Blue Sky Press in 2013.

ISBN 978-0-545-78573-0

12 11 10 9 8 7 6 5 4 3 2 1   14 15 16 17 18 19/0

Printed in the U.S.A.   08

This edition first printing, September 2014

Designed by Kathleen Westray

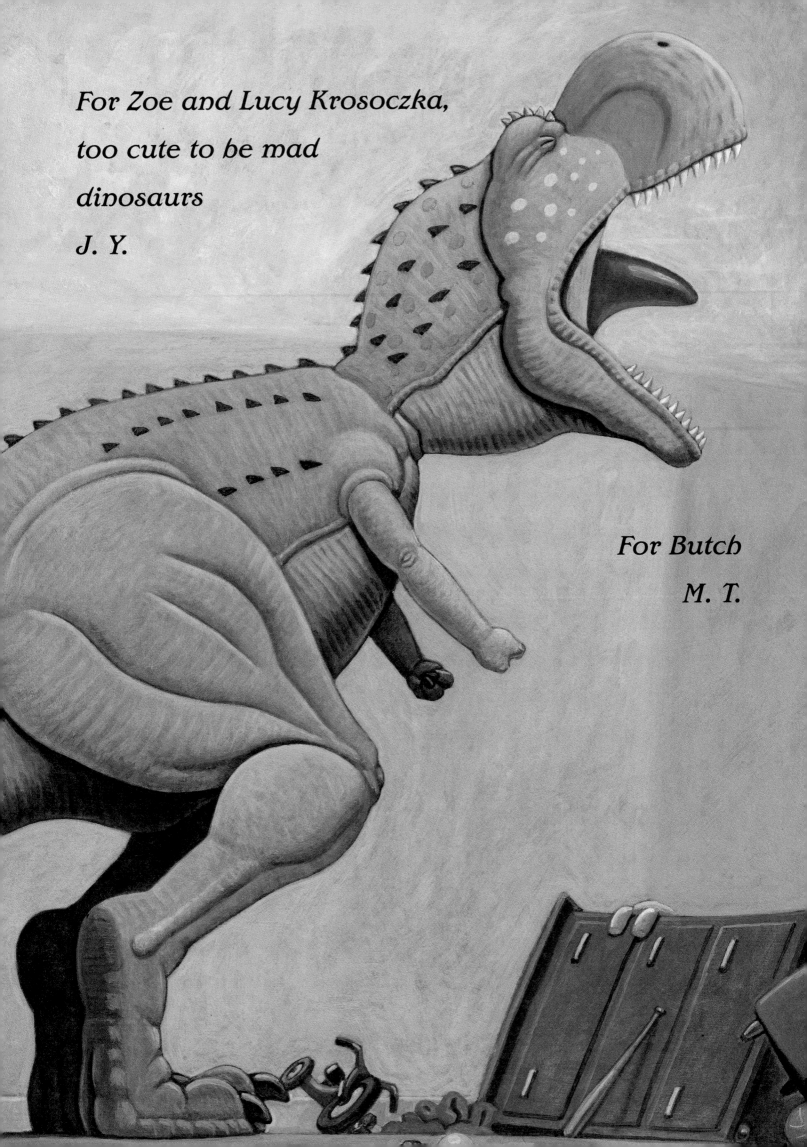

For Zoe and Lucy Krosoczka,
too cute to be mad
dinosaurs
J. Y.

For Butch
M. T.

How does a dinosaur act
when he's mad?

Does he roar,

slam the door,

yell at Mom

or at Dad?

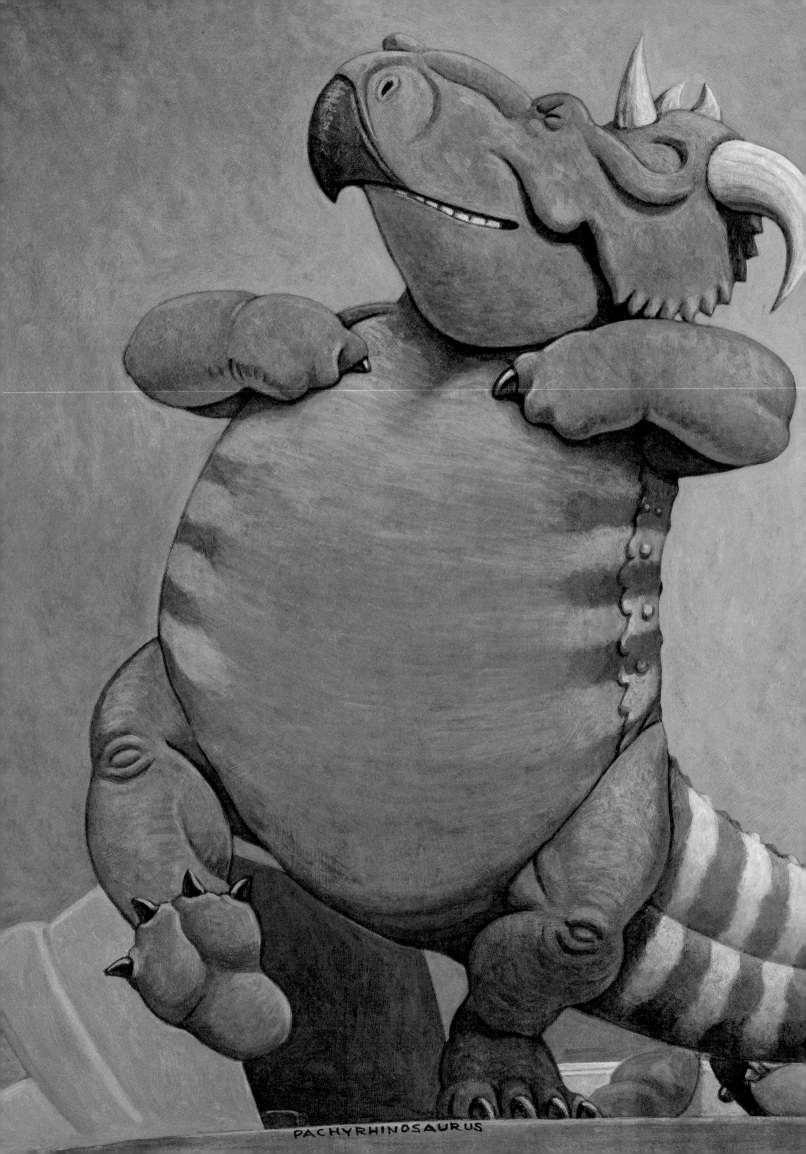

PACHYRHINOSAURUS

When he can't get his way,

does he boast, "I'll be bad!"

Is that what dinosaurs say

when they're mad?

When Papa says, "No!"
does he grumble
and pout?

When Mama says, "No!"

does he throw

toys about?

When he's told
to sit still,
does he kick

at a chair?

Does he act as if
Mother and Father
aren't there?

When he hears, "Take a nap!"
does he give dirty looks?
When he's told, "Quiet down!"
does he rip up his books?

No cookies today?

Fling a mug

at the cat!

"Time for bed!"
Does he bang on the floor
with his bat?

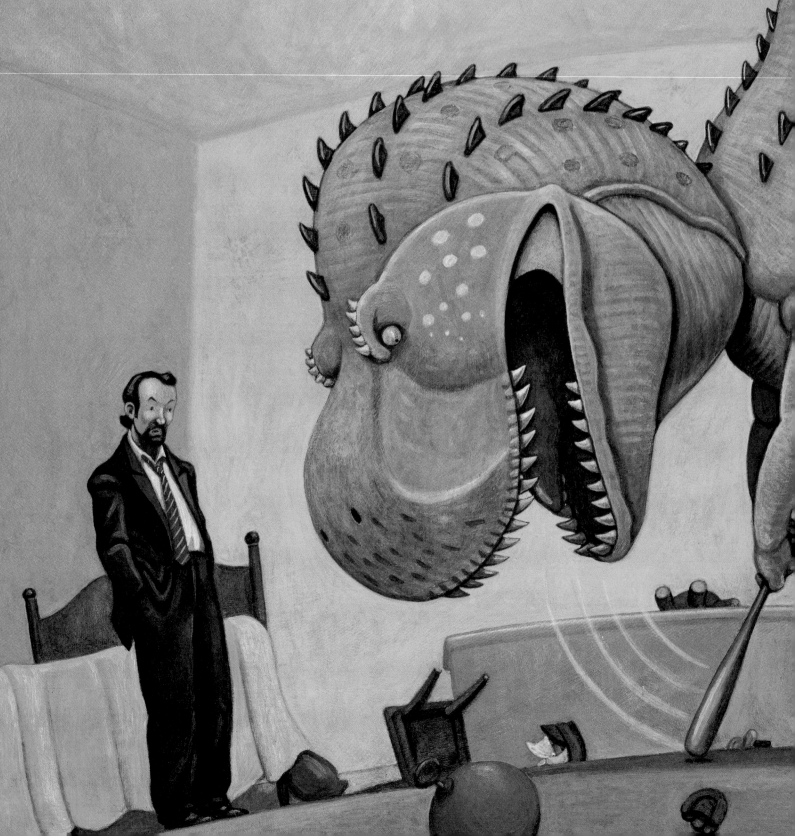

No . . .
a dinosaur
doesn't—

he counts up to ten,

then after a time out,

breathes calmly . . .

and then . . .

he cleans up his mess,
and he picks up
the mug.

He says,
"I'm so sorry."
He gives
a big hug.

His anger is gone,

so he opens the door.

Not mad? I'm so glad,

little dinosaur.